BEYOND CLICKS

THE ART AND SCIENCE OF PERFORMANCE MARKETING

VIKAS KRISHNA KUMAR JAIN

To all the digital marketing enthusiasts who thrive in the fast-paced, dynamic digital world of performance marketing. This book is for those who look beyond clicks and aim for real results.

And to my incredible family and friends, your support and encouragement have been my constant source of strength. Thank you for always being there!

Special thanks to my loving son, Ranbir, who always motivates me to write more, and to my cute dog, Bruno, my best companion. You both bring joy and inspiration to my life every day.

Bruno and I

Contents

Foreword

It is with great pleasure that I introduce Beyond Clicks: Mastering the Art and Science of Performance Marketing. This book, written by Vikas Krishan Kumar Jain, My Friend & a seasoned expert in the field, offers a comprehensive guide to navigating the complexities of performance marketing. Vikas has distilled his years of experience and insights into this book, providing readers with practical strategies, real-world examples, and actionable advice that can transform their marketing efforts.

The highlight of this book is the Precision Persona Strategy, a unique approach developed by Vikas that has consistently delivered outstanding results for his clients. By meticulously defining and targeting the right audience with tailored content and outreach efforts, this strategy goes beyond mere clicks to achieve genuine engagement and measurable outcomes.

Fabian Dech
Incredible Good Guy
Haarlem, North Holland, Netherlands

Fabian Dech

ppp

Beyond Clicks....

We all know that as digital marketers, we are in a very dynamic digital domain. Hence, it is no longer sufficient to simply generate clicks and traffic. The true measure of success lies in what happens beyond the click – the actions users take, the conversions achieved, and the return on investment (ROI) realized. This is the essence of performance marketing.

Performance marketing goes beyond surface-level metrics, delving into the entire journey of the visitor. By understanding this journey, marketers can gain invaluable insights that optimize the performance of their paid marketing investments. It's about motivating the user to perform the desired action, whether it's making a purchase, signing up for a newsletter, or downloading an app.

For agencies, this means focusing on what their clients are truly achieving through their campaigns. Are these campaigns delivering measurable results? Are they enhancing the client's bottom line? By concentrating on ROI, agencies can ensure their efforts are not just creating noise but driving meaningful outcomes.

In today's fast-paced marketing domain, traditional methods are increasingly giving way to performance marketing. To survive and thrive, marketers must embrace this shift. Performance marketing provides a data-driven approach that offers greater accountability, precision, and efficiency.

This book, **Beyond Clicks: Mastering the Art and Science of Performance Marketing,** provides deep insights into running successful performance marketing campaigns. Drawing on the extensive experience of Vikas Krishan Kumar Jain, a seasoned expert in the field, this guide offers practical strategies and real-world examples to help you navigate the complexities of performance marketing and achieve remarkable results.

vikas jain

Vikas Jain

BEYOND CLICKS....

• x •

The Precision Persona Strategy-pps

Introduction

As we all digital marketers know, the digital marketing domain is incredibly dynamic., where results-driven approaches are paramount, having a unique and effective strategy is crucial. One such innovative approach is the Precision Persona Strategy. Developed by **Vikas Krishan Kumar Jain,** this strategy has consistently delivered outstanding results for numerous clients by meticulously defining and targeting the right audience with tailored content and outreach efforts.

Defining the Target Audience

The first step in the Precision Persona Strategy is to define the target audience for the services being offered. This involves a thorough analysis of existing client data to understand who becomes a customer and their journey from awareness to conversion.

Analyzing Existing Client Data:

- Identify key demographics and psychographics of current customers.
- Map out the customer journey stages – from awareness, consideration, decision, to retention.

Defining Personas:

- Create detailed personas representing different segments of the target audience.
- Each persona should include demographics, job roles, pain points, goals, and preferred communication channels.

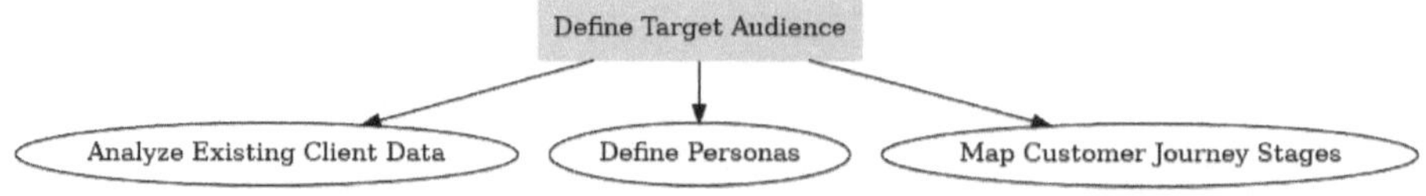

Defining Target Personas

Understanding Pain Areas and Objectives

To resonate with the target audience, it is crucial to understand their pain areas and objectives. This can be achieved by putting oneself in their shoes and leveraging past interactions and feedback.

Empathy Mapping:

- Develop empathy maps to gain insights into the target personas' thoughts, feelings, and actions.
- Probing Outsourcing Experiences:
- Conduct interviews or surveys with current and past clients to gather insights on their experiences with outsourcing agencies in India.
- Identify common pain points and challenges they faced.

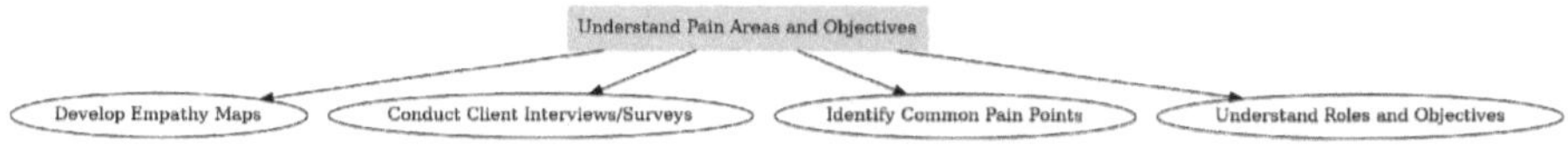

Understanding Pain Areas and Objectives

Crafting the Content Strategy

With a clear understanding of the target audience and their pain points, the next step is to craft a content strategy that addresses these issues and positions the agency as the ultimate solution provider.

Content Themes:

- Focus on pain areas and solutions.
- Highlight the agency's commitment to addressing these issues and ensuring client satisfaction.

Content Types:

- Blog posts, case studies, whitepapers, and videos that showcase success stories and problem-solving capabilities.
- Personalized emails and LinkedIn messages addressing specific pain points.

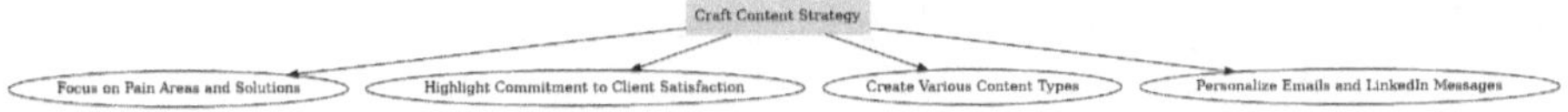

Crafting the Content Strategy

Implementing the Precision Persona Strategy

With the content strategy in place, it's time to implement the Precision Persona Strategy. This involves creating targeted campaigns and coordinated outreach efforts across various platforms.

Preparing the Target List:

- Compile a list of target agencies, including 100 potential clients at a time.
- Gather details such as agency size, email addresses, phone numbers, LinkedIn URLs, and key decision-makers.

LinkedIn Campaign:

- Create a LinkedIn campaign focusing on the defined agencies and personas.
- Use targeted ads and sponsored content to reach these specific audiences.

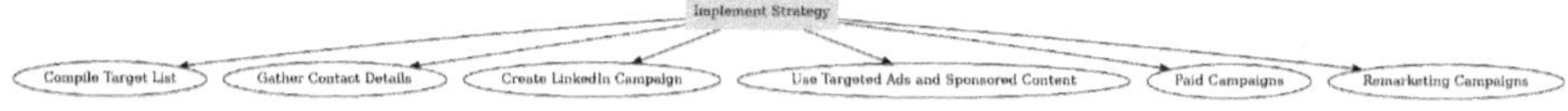

Implementing the Precision Persona Strategy

Coordinated Outreach

A multi-channel approach ensures comprehensive coverage and maximizes the chances of engagement and conversion.

LinkedIn Outreach:

Have the outreach team contact prospects on LinkedIn, sending personalized connection requests and messages.

Email Marketing:

The email marketing team sends personalized mailers to the defined list, highlighting solutions to their pain points and success stories.

Social Media Engagement:

The Social Media Manager plans content calendars and posts that align with the campaign themes.

Use targeted hashtags, callouts, and engagement tactics to reach the audience.

Retargeting Campaigns:

Implement retargeting campaigns for website traffic from the same regions to maintain top-of-mind awareness and follow up with visitors.

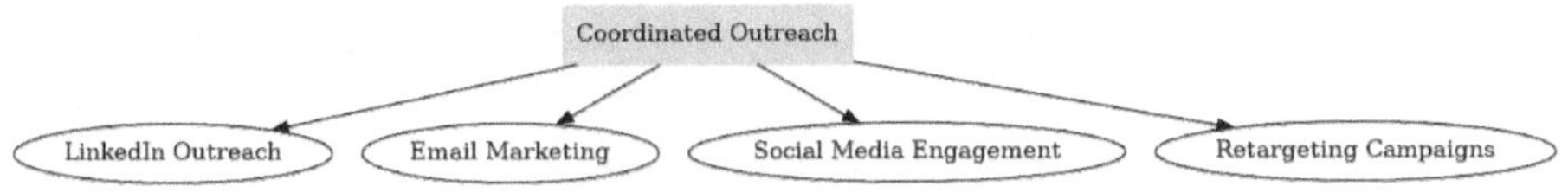

Coordinated Outreach

Achieving Desired Actions and Brand Recall

By executing the Precision Persona Strategy, the desired actions from the target audience are achieved, and the brand's recall value is significantly enhanced.

Measuring Success:

Track key metrics such as engagement rates, conversion rates, and ROI to measure the success of the campaigns.

Continuous Optimization:

Continuously analyze campaign performance and make data-driven adjustments to optimize results.

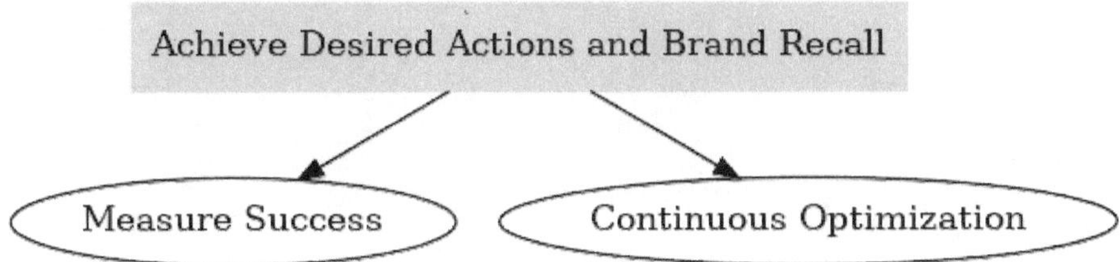

Achieving Desired Actions and Brand Recall

Conclusion

The Precision Persona Strategy is a comprehensive and highly effective approach to performance marketing. By meticulously defining the target audience, understanding their pain points, crafting tailored content, and executing coordinated outreach efforts, marketers can achieve outstanding results. This strategy not only drives desired actions but also enhances brand recall and loyalty, ensuring long-term success.

ONE

THE FOUNDATIONS OF PERFORMANCE MARKETING

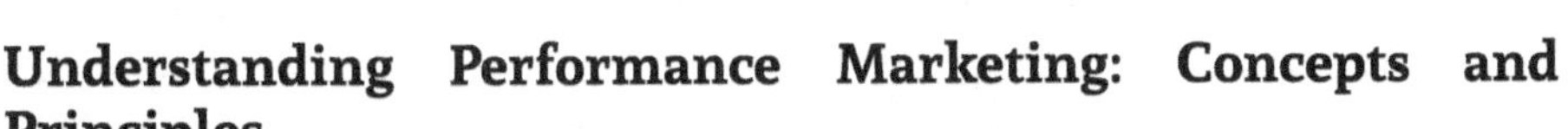

Understanding Performance Marketing: Concepts and Principles

Performance marketing is a comprehensive term that describes online marketing and advertising programs where advertisers pay when a specific action occurs. Actions include, but are not limited to, clicks, sales, leads, or any other measurable metric. Unlike traditional advertising, performance marketing is centered on measurable outcomes.

The principles of performance marketing are rooted in accountability and measurability. Every aspect of a campaign can be tracked, analyzed, and optimized for better results. This chapter introduces the key concepts and principles that underpin performance marketing, providing a solid foundation for understanding the rest of the book.

Key Concepts of Performance Marketing:

Measurable Results:

At the heart of performance marketing is the ability to measure every action taken by a user. This data-driven approach allows marketers to track the performance of their campaigns accurately.

Example: Dentsu Webchutney, an Indian digital agency, ran a campaign for Flipkart during the Big Billion Days sale. They used advanced tracking tools to measure each click, add-to-cart action, and purchase, allowing them to optimize the campaign in real-time and significantly increase sales.

Cost Per Action (CPA):

One of the main pricing models in performance marketing is CPA, where advertisers only pay when a specified action is completed. This model ensures that marketing budgets are spent efficiently.

Example: An Indian agency, iProspect India, managed a CPA campaign for HDFC Bank's new credit card sign-ups. They only paid for each successful sign-up, ensuring that the marketing spend directly contributed to acquiring new customers.

Accountability:

Performance marketing holds advertisers accountable for delivering measurable results. Campaigns are continuously monitored and optimized to ensure the highest possible return on investment (ROI).

Example: Interactive Avenues, a digital marketing agency in India, worked with Standard Chartered to increase online loan applications. By focusing on measurable outcomes and regular optimization, they achieved a high ROI and significantly boosted the bank's online application numbers.

Optimization:

Continuous improvement is a hallmark of performance marketing. Campaigns are regularly analyzed, and strategies are adjusted to maximize performance.

Example: Social Beat, an Indian digital agency, optimized a performance marketing campaign for Swiggy, a food delivery app. By analyzing user behavior and adjusting ad creatives and targeting, they improved conversion rates and reduced acquisition costs.

Principles of Performance Marketing:

Data-Driven Decision Making:

Decisions are based on data analysis and insights. Performance marketers rely on metrics and KPIs to guide their strategies and ensure they are achieving their goals.

Example: Performics India used data-driven strategies to manage a campaign for Lenovo. They analyzed customer data to tailor ads and offers, leading to a significant increase in online sales.

Targeting and Segmentation:

Successful performance marketing campaigns target specific audiences. Marketers use segmentation to deliver personalized messages to the right people at the right time.

Example: WatConsult, an Indian digital agency, segmented audiences for their client, Mahindra Holidays, based on browsing behavior and past interactions. This targeted approach resulted in higher engagement and conversion rates.

Conversion Focus:

The ultimate goal of performance marketing is to drive conversions. Whether it's making a purchase, signing up for a newsletter, or downloading an app, every campaign is designed to encourage users to take a specific action.

Example: GroupM India focused on driving app downloads for a global tech company. Their performance marketing strategy centered on high-converting ad formats and precise targeting, significantly boosting the number of downloads.

Scalability:

Performance marketing campaigns are scalable. Once a campaign is proven to be successful, it can be expanded to reach a larger audience and generate more conversions.

Example: Kinnect, an Indian digital agency, successfully scaled a campaign for Amazon India during the festive season. After initial success with a small audience, they expanded the campaign to reach millions, resulting in a substantial increase in sales.

Key Metrics and KPIs for Performance-Based Campaigns

To measure the success of performance marketing campaigns, marketers rely on a variety of metrics and key performance indicators (KPIs). These metrics provide valuable insights into how well a campaign is performing and where improvements can be made.

Common Metrics in Performance Marketing:

Click-Through Rate (CTR):

CTR measures the number of clicks an ad receives divided by the number of times it is shown. A higher CTR indicates that the ad is relevant and compelling to the audience.

Example: Mirum India ran a campaign for a global fashion brand. By optimizing ad creatives and targeting, they improved the CTR, leading to increased website traffic and sales.

Conversion Rate:

The conversion rate is the percentage of users who complete a desired action after clicking on an ad. This metric is crucial for understanding the effectiveness of a campaign.

Example: WATConsult worked with Tata Motors to boost test drive bookings through a digital campaign. By optimizing the landing pages and ad creatives, they increased the conversion rate significantly.

Cost Per Click (CPC):

CPC is the amount an advertiser pays each time a user clicks on their ad. It helps marketers understand the cost-effectiveness of their campaigns.

Example: Performics India managed a CPC campaign for a global electronics brand. By optimizing keywords and ad placements, they reduced the CPC while maintaining high ad visibility.

Cost Per Acquisition (CPA):

CPA measures the cost of acquiring a customer who completes a specific action. This metric is essential for evaluating the ROI of a campaign.

Example: Social Beat ran a CPA campaign for a leading e-commerce platform in India. They focused on reducing the CPA by optimizing ad targeting and creatives, resulting in a lower acquisition cost and higher ROI.

Return on Ad Spend (ROAS):

ROAS is the revenue generated from an ad campaign divided by the cost of the campaign. It provides insight into the overall profitability of the advertising efforts.

Example: GroupM India achieved a high ROAS for a global tech company by running targeted ads and continuously optimizing the campaign based on performance data.

KPIs for Performance Marketing:

Lead Generation:

The number of leads generated from a campaign is a key KPI for performance marketing. Leads are potential customers who have shown interest in a product or service.

Example: Interactive Avenues generated a significant number of leads for a financial services company by using targeted ad campaigns and optimized landing pages.

Sales Revenue:

Sales revenue is a critical KPI for e-commerce and other businesses focused on driving sales. It measures the total revenue generated from a campaign.

Example: iProspect India increased sales revenue for a global fashion retailer by implementing a performance marketing strategy that included targeted ads and promotional offers.

Customer Lifetime Value (CLV):

CLV is the total revenue expected from a customer over their lifetime. It helps marketers understand the long-term value of acquiring a customer.

Example: Dentsu Webchutney worked with a subscription-based service to increase CLV by focusing on customer retention and upselling strategies.

Return on Investment (ROI):

ROI measures the overall profitability of a campaign. It compares the revenue generated to the cost of the campaign to determine its success.

Example: Kinnect achieved a high ROI for an FMCG brand by running a well-targeted and optimized performance marketing campaign that drove significant sales.

Performance Marketing vs. Traditional Marketing

Performance marketing differs significantly from traditional marketing approaches. While traditional marketing focuses on brand awareness and reach, performance marketing is centered on measurable outcomes and accountability.

Key Differences:

Measurability:

Traditional marketing relies on metrics like impressions and reach, which can be difficult to quantify in terms of direct impact. Performance marketing, on the other hand, measures specific actions and conversions.

Example: An Indian agency ran a traditional marketing campaign for a global car manufacturer, focusing on TV ads and print media. While it increased brand awareness, the direct impact on sales was hard to measure. In contrast, their performance marketing campaign for the same client focused on driving online test drive bookings and provided clear, measurable results.

Cost Structure:

Traditional marketing often involves upfront costs with no guarantee of results. Performance marketing uses a pay-for-performance model, where advertisers pay only when a specific action is completed.

Example: Performics India managed a traditional marketing campaign for a global FMCG brand, spending a fixed budget on TV and radio ads. They also ran a performance marketing campaign with a CPA model, ensuring the client paid only for actual sales generated, resulting in a more cost-effective strategy.

Accountability:

Performance marketing holds marketers accountable for delivering results. Every aspect of a campaign is tracked and optimized to ensure the highest possible ROI.

Example: Interactive Avenues ran a performance marketing campaign for a fintech company, using advanced tracking tools to monitor every user action. This level of accountability allowed them to optimize the campaign in real-time and deliver a high ROI.

Flexibility:

Performance marketing campaigns can be quickly adjusted based on real-time data and insights. Traditional marketing campaigns, such as print ads or TV commercials, are less flexible and more difficult to modify once they are launched.

Example: WATConsult managed a performance marketing campaign for an Indian e-commerce platform, allowing them to make rapid adjustments based on real-time data, whereas their traditional marketing campaign for the same client had to run its course before any changes could be made.

Advantages of Performance Marketing:

Efficiency:

Performance marketing ensures that marketing budgets are spent efficiently, as advertisers only pay for completed actions.

Example: GroupM India ran a highly efficient performance marketing campaign for a global airline, focusing on ticket bookings. They achieved a low CPA, ensuring that the marketing spend directly contributed to sales.

Targeted Approach:

Marketers can use advanced targeting and segmentation techniques to reach specific audiences with personalized messages.

Example: Mirum India used sophisticated targeting techniques to reach specific demographics for a global beauty brand, resulting in higher engagement and conversion rates.

Real-Time Optimization:

Campaigns can be continuously monitored and optimized to improve performance and achieve better results.

Example: Social Beat continuously optimized a campaign for a food delivery app, making real-time adjustments to ad creatives and targeting based on performance data, leading to improved results.

Scalability:

Performance marketing campaigns can be scaled to reach a larger audience and generate more conversions once proven successful.

Example: iProspect India successfully scaled a performance marketing campaign for an international travel agency, initially targeting a small audience and then expanding to a global scale after seeing positive results.

TWO
ADVANCED PPC STRATEGIES

Google Ads: Tips for Optimizing Ad Performance

Google Ads is a powerful tool for performance marketers, offering a wide range of features to optimize ad performance. Understanding how to use these features effectively can significantly enhance the success of your campaigns.

Tips for Optimizing Google Ads:

Keyword Research:

Conduct thorough keyword research to identify the most relevant and high-performing keywords for your campaigns.

Example: Dentsu Webchutney optimized a Google Ads campaign for an international travel agency by using advanced keyword research tools to identify high-intent keywords, resulting in increased click-through rates and conversions.

Ad Copy Optimization:

Write compelling ad copy that includes relevant keywords and a strong call-to-action.

Example: Interactive Avenues optimized ad copy for a global electronics brand, focusing on highlighting key product features and benefits. This approach led to higher engagement and improved conversion rates.

Bid Management:

Use automated bidding strategies to optimize bids for maximum performance.

Example: Performics India used automated bidding strategies to manage a Google Ads campaign for a global FMCG brand, ensuring optimal bid adjustments based on real-time performance data.

Ad Extensions:

Utilize ad extensions to provide additional information and increase ad visibility.

Example: Social Beat implemented ad extensions for a food delivery app, including sitelink extensions and call extensions, leading to higher click-through rates and better user engagement.

A/B Testing:

Continuously test different ad variations to determine which performs best.

Example: iProspect India conducted A/B testing for a global fashion retailer, experimenting with different ad creatives and messaging to identify the most effective combination.

Bing Ads and Alternative Platforms

While Google Ads is the most popular PPC platform, Bing Ads and other alternative platforms also offer valuable opportunities for performance marketers. These platforms can provide access to different audiences and often have lower competition.

Optimizing Bing Ads:

Leverage Unique Features:

Bing Ads offers unique features such as LinkedIn profile targeting, which can be particularly useful for B2B campaigns.

Example: Performics India used LinkedIn profile targeting in Bing Ads for a B2B software company, resulting in more precise targeting and higher conversion rates.

Importing Google Ads Campaigns:

Utilize the ability to import Google Ads campaigns into Bing Ads to save time and maintain consistency.

Example: iProspect India imported a successful Google Ads campaign into Bing Ads for an international travel agency, achieving similar success on both platforms.

Adjust Bids Based on Performance:

Regularly adjust bids based on performance data to ensure optimal ad placement.

Example: Interactive Avenues managed bid adjustments for a global electronics brand on Bing Ads, optimizing bids based on performance metrics to achieve better ROI.

Alternative PPC Platforms:

Amazon Advertising:

For e-commerce businesses, Amazon Advertising can be a powerful platform to reach potential customers.

Example: Social Beat managed an Amazon Advertising campaign for a global beauty brand, focusing on product display ads and sponsored product ads, resulting in increased sales and visibility.

Facebook Ads:

Facebook Ads offers advanced targeting options and a wide range of ad formats.

Example: Dentsu Webchutney optimized a Facebook Ads campaign for a global fashion brand, using detailed audience targeting and dynamic ads to drive conversions.

LinkedIn Ads:

LinkedIn Ads is ideal for B2B marketing, offering precise targeting based on professional attributes.

Example: GroupM India ran a successful LinkedIn Ads campaign for a global tech company, targeting decision-makers and professionals in specific industries.

Remarketing and Retargeting Techniques

Remarketing and retargeting are powerful strategies in performance marketing, allowing you to re-engage users who have previously interacted with your brand. These techniques can significantly improve conversion rates by targeting users who are already familiar with your products or services.

Remarketing Strategies:

Dynamic Remarketing:

Show personalized ads based on the products or services users have viewed on your website.

Example: Interactive Avenues implemented dynamic remarketing for a global electronics brand, displaying personalized ads featuring products users had previously viewed. This approach led to higher engagement and conversions.

Segmented Remarketing Lists:

Create segmented remarketing lists based on user behavior, such as past purchases or time spent on the website.

Example: Social Beat segmented remarketing lists for a food delivery app, targeting users who had abandoned their carts with personalized offers. This strategy increased conversion rates and reduced cart abandonment.

Cross-Platform Remarketing:

Utilize cross-platform remarketing to reach users across multiple channels, such as Google Ads and Facebook Ads.

Example: iProspect India ran cross-platform remarketing campaigns for a global fashion retailer, ensuring consistent messaging and increased visibility across different platforms.

Retargeting Techniques:

Pixel-Based Retargeting:

Use tracking pixels to target users based on their behavior on your website.

Example: Performics India implemented pixel-based retargeting for a B2B software company, targeting users who had visited specific product pages with relevant ads.

Email Retargeting:

Retarget users through email campaigns based on their interactions with your website or previous emails.

Example: Dentsu Webchutney used email retargeting for a subscription-based service, sending personalized emails to users who had shown interest but not completed a subscription.

Lookalike Audiences:

Create lookalike audiences based on your best-performing customers to reach new potential customers with similar characteristics.

Example: GroupM India created lookalike audiences for a global tech company, expanding their reach and driving new user acquisitions.

THREE

Affiliate Marketing Mastery

Building and Managing an Affiliate Program

Affiliate marketing is a performance-based marketing strategy where affiliates earn a commission for driving actions, such as sales or leads, through their marketing efforts. Building and managing a successful affiliate program requires careful planning and execution.

Building an Affiliate Program:

Define Program Goals:

Clearly define the goals of your affiliate program, such as increasing sales, generating leads, or expanding brand awareness.

Example: Interactive Avenues defined clear goals for an affiliate program for a global fashion retailer, focusing on driving online sales through affiliate partnerships.

Choose the Right Platform:

Select an affiliate marketing platform that offers robust tracking, reporting, and management features.

Example: Performics India used a leading affiliate marketing platform to manage a program for a global electronics brand, ensuring accurate tracking and seamless management.

Create Attractive Commission Structures:

Offer competitive commission rates and incentives to attract high-quality affiliates.

Example: Social Beat designed an attractive commission structure for an affiliate program for a food delivery app, including tiered commissions and performance-based bonuses.

Managing an Affiliate Program:

Recruiting High-Quality Affiliates:

Identify and recruit affiliates who align with your brand and have the potential to drive significant traffic and conversions.

Example: iProspect India recruited high-quality affiliates for a global fashion retailer, focusing on influencers and content creators with a strong online presence.

Providing Marketing Resources:

Offer affiliates a range of marketing resources, such as banners, links, and content, to help them promote your products effectively.

Example: Dentsu Webchutney provided comprehensive marketing resources for affiliates promoting a subscription-based service, including custom banners and email templates.

Tracking and Attribution:

Implement robust tracking and attribution systems to accurately measure affiliate performance and allocate commissions.

Example: GroupM India used advanced tracking tools to manage an affiliate program for a global tech company, ensuring accurate attribution and timely commission payments.

Communication and Support:

Maintain regular communication with affiliates and provide ongoing support to help them succeed.

Example: Interactive Avenues established a dedicated support team for affiliates in their program for a global fashion retailer, offering training and assistance to maximize performance.

Strategies for Recruiting High-Quality Affiliates

Recruiting high-quality affiliates is crucial for the success of your affiliate program. These affiliates can drive significant traffic and conversions, contributing to the overall growth of your business.

Recruitment Strategies:

Targeted Outreach:

Identify potential affiliates who align with your brand and have a strong online presence. Reach out to them with personalized offers.

Example: Social Beat used targeted outreach to recruit influencers and content creators for an affiliate program for a food delivery app. This approach resulted in high-quality partnerships and increased conversions.

Affiliate Networks:

Join affiliate networks to access a broader pool of potential affiliates and simplify the recruitment process.

Example: Performics India joined a leading affiliate network to manage a program for a global electronics brand, leveraging the network's extensive affiliate base to drive traffic and sales.

Incentives and Bonuses:

Offer incentives and bonuses to attract top-performing affiliates and motivate them to promote your products.

Example: iProspect India offered performance-based bonuses to affiliates in their program for a global fashion retailer, encouraging higher levels of promotion and engagement.

Content Collaboration:

Collaborate with potential affiliates on content creation, such as guest posts, reviews, or sponsored content.

Example: Dentsu Webchutney collaborated with influencers and bloggers to create content promoting a subscription-based service, driving traffic and conversions through authentic recommendations.

Referral Programs:

Implement a referral program to encourage existing affiliates to recruit new affiliates.

Example: GroupM India introduced a referral program for an affiliate program for a global tech company, offering commission bonuses to affiliates who referred new partners.

Tracking, Attribution, and Payment Models

Effective tracking, accurate attribution, and transparent payment models are essential components of a successful affiliate program. These elements ensure that affiliates are rewarded fairly and that the program operates smoothly.

Tracking and Attribution:

Tracking Tools:

Use robust tracking tools to monitor affiliate performance and measure the effectiveness of their marketing efforts.

Example: Interactive Avenues implemented advanced tracking tools for an affiliate program for a global fashion retailer, ensuring accurate measurement of clicks, leads, and sales.

Attribution Models:

Choose an attribution model that accurately reflects the contributions of affiliates to conversions, such as last-click, first-click, or multi-touch attribution.

Example: Performics India used a multi-touch attribution model for an affiliate program for a global electronics brand, providing a comprehensive view of the customer journey and the impact of affiliate marketing.

Real-Time Reporting:

Provide affiliates with real-time reporting to give them insights into their performance and help them optimize their campaigns.

Example: Social Beat offered real-time reporting for affiliates in their program for a food delivery app, enabling affiliates to track their performance and make data-driven decisions.

Payment Models:

Cost Per Sale (CPS):

Pay affiliates a commission based on the sales they generate. This model aligns incentives and ensures that marketing spend is directly tied to revenue.

Example: iProspect India used a CPS model for an affiliate program for a global fashion retailer, paying commissions based on the value of sales driven by affiliates.

Cost Per Lead (CPL):

Pay affiliates for generating leads, such as sign-ups or form submissions. This model is effective for businesses focused on lead generation.

Example: Dentsu Webchutney used a CPL model for an affiliate program for a subscription-based service, paying commissions for each new subscriber acquired through affiliates.

Cost Per Click (CPC):

Pay affiliates for each click generated. This model is less common but can be useful for driving traffic to a website.

Example: GroupM India used a CPC model for an affiliate program for a global tech company, paying affiliates for driving traffic to the company's landing pages.

Hybrid Models:

Combine multiple payment models to create a hybrid approach that rewards affiliates for different types of actions.

Example: Interactive Avenues used a hybrid model for an affiliate program for a global fashion retailer, combining CPS and CPL to incentivize both sales and lead generation.

FOUR

Conversion Rate Optimization (CRO)

Techniques for Optimizing Landing Pages

Conversion rate optimization (CRO) focuses on improving the percentage of visitors who complete a desired action on your website, such as making a purchase or filling out a form. Optimizing landing pages is a crucial aspect of CRO.

Landing Page Optimization Techniques:

Clear Call-to-Action (CTA):

Ensure that your landing pages have a clear and compelling call-to-action that guides visitors towards the desired action.

Example: Social Beat optimized landing pages for a food delivery app by simplifying the design and highlighting the CTA, resulting in higher conversion rates.

A/B Testing:

Conduct A/B testing to compare different versions of a landing page and identify which one performs better.

Example: Performics India conducted A/B testing for a global electronics brand, experimenting with different headlines, images, and CTAs to determine the most effective combination.

Load Speed Optimization:

Improve the load speed of your landing pages to reduce bounce rates and enhance the user experience.

Example: Interactive Avenues optimized the load speed of landing pages for a global fashion retailer, leading to lower bounce rates and higher conversion rates.

Responsive Design:

Ensure that your landing pages are mobile-friendly and provide a seamless experience across all devices.

Example: iProspect India implemented responsive design for landing pages for a global fashion retailer, ensuring a consistent user experience on both desktop and mobile devices.

Social Proof:

Incorporate social proof, such as testimonials, reviews, and case studies, to build trust and credibility.

Example: Dentsu Webchutney added customer testimonials and reviews to landing pages for a subscription-based service, increasing trust and conversions.

A/B Testing and Multivariate Testing Methods

A/B testing and multivariate testing are essential techniques in CRO, allowing you to experiment with different elements of your landing pages and identify the most effective combinations.

A/B Testing:

Single Variable Testing:

Test one variable at a time, such as the headline, image, or CTA, to determine its impact on conversion rates.

Example: Social Beat conducted A/B testing for a food delivery app, comparing different CTAs to identify the most effective one for driving conversions.

Statistical Significance:

Ensure that your A/B tests run long enough to achieve statistical significance and produce reliable results.

Example: Performics India ran A/B tests for a global electronics brand until they reached statistical significance, ensuring that the results were accurate and actionable.

Iterative Testing:

Continuously test and optimize different elements of your landing pages to achieve incremental improvements.

Example: Interactive Avenues implemented iterative A/B testing for a global fashion retailer, regularly testing and optimizing various elements to improve conversion rates over time.

Multivariate Testing:

Multiple Variable Testing:

Test multiple variables simultaneously to understand their combined impact on conversion rates.

Example: iProspect India conducted multivariate testing for a global fashion retailer, experimenting with different combinations of headlines, images, and CTAs to identify the best-performing layout.

Complex Interaction Analysis:

Analyze the interactions between different variables to understand how they influence each other and affect overall performance.

Example: Dentsu Webchutney used multivariate testing for a subscription-based service, analyzing the interactions between various page elements to optimize the overall user experience.

Advanced Testing Tools:

Utilize advanced testing tools and software to manage and analyze multivariate tests effectively.

Example: GroupM India used advanced multivariate testing tools to optimize landing pages for a global tech company, providing detailed insights into the performance of different page elements.

Tools and Technologies for CRO

Leveraging the right tools and technologies is essential for effective CRO. These tools help you analyze user behavior, conduct tests, and implement changes to improve conversion rates.

CRO Tools and Technologies:

Google Optimize:

A free tool from Google that allows you to conduct A/B tests, multivariate tests, and redirect tests on your website.

Example: Performics India used Google Optimize to run A/B tests for a global electronics brand, optimizing various elements of their landing pages to improve conversion rates.

Hotjar:

A comprehensive tool that provides heatmaps, session recordings, and surveys to analyze user behavior and identify areas for improvement.

Example: Social Beat used Hotjar to gather insights into user behavior on landing pages for a food delivery app, implementing changes based on heatmap data to enhance the user experience.

Optimizely:

A powerful experimentation platform that offers advanced A/B testing, multivariate testing, and personalization features.

Example: Interactive Avenues used Optimizely to run multivariate tests for a global fashion retailer, identifying the most effective combinations of page elements to maximize conversions.

VWO (Visual Website Optimizer):

A versatile CRO platform that provides A/B testing, multivariate testing, and user insights to optimize your website for conversions.

Example: iProspect India used VWO to conduct A/B tests for a global fashion retailer, optimizing their landing pages to achieve higher conversion rates.

Crazy Egg:

A tool that offers heatmaps, scrollmaps, and A/B testing features to help you understand user behavior and optimize your website.

Example: Dentsu Webchutney used Crazy Egg to analyze user interactions on landing pages for a subscription-based service, implementing changes based on heatmap data to improve conversions.

FIVE

DATA-DRIVEN DECISION MAKING

Leveraging Analytics for Performance Marketing

Data-driven decision making is crucial for performance marketing, allowing you to base your strategies on solid data and insights. Leveraging analytics helps you understand user behavior, measure campaign performance, and optimize your marketing efforts.

Analytics Tools and Techniques:

Google Analytics:

A comprehensive tool that provides detailed insights into website traffic, user behavior, and conversion rates.

Example: Performics India used Google Analytics to track and analyze the performance of a digital campaign for a global electronics brand, making data-driven adjustments to improve results.

Adobe Analytics:

An advanced analytics platform that offers real-time data, segmentation, and predictive analytics to optimize marketing strategies.

Example: Interactive Avenues used Adobe Analytics to manage a performance marketing campaign for a global fashion retailer, leveraging predictive analytics to anticipate user behavior and drive conversions.

Custom Dashboards:

Create custom dashboards to visualize key metrics and track the performance of your campaigns in real-time.

Example: iProspect India developed custom dashboards for a global fashion retailer, providing real-time insights into campaign performance and enabling quick adjustments based on data.

Attribution Modeling:

Use attribution models to understand the contribution of different marketing channels and touchpoints to conversions.

Example: Dentsu Webchutney implemented multi-touch attribution modeling for a subscription-based service, gaining insights into the customer journey and optimizing marketing spend across channels.

Advanced Tools for Data Collection and Analysis

Advanced tools for data collection and analysis enable performance marketers to gather comprehensive data, gain deeper insights, and make more informed decisions.

Advanced Data Collection Tools:

Google Tag Manager:

A tag management system that allows you to manage and deploy marketing tags on your website without modifying the code.

Example: Social Beat used Google Tag Manager to streamline the implementation of tracking tags for a food delivery app, ensuring accurate data collection and reducing the need for developer support.

Heap Analytics:

An analytics platform that automatically captures every user interaction on your website, providing detailed insights into user behavior.

Example: Performics India used Heap Analytics to track user interactions on landing pages for a global electronics brand, identifying key behaviors that led to conversions.

Mixpanel:

A powerful analytics tool that focuses on user behavior and engagement, offering advanced segmentation and funnel analysis.

Example: Interactive Avenues used Mixpanel to analyze user behavior for a global fashion retailer, optimizing marketing strategies based on detailed insights into user interactions.

Advanced Data Analysis Tools:

Tableau:

A data visualization tool that allows you to create interactive and shareable dashboards, providing insights into complex data sets.

Example: iProspect India used Tableau to visualize data for a global fashion retailer, creating interactive dashboards that helped stakeholders understand campaign performance and make data-driven decisions.

R and Python:

Programming languages that offer powerful data analysis and visualization capabilities, enabling advanced statistical analysis and machine learning.

Example: Dentsu Webchutney used Python to analyze large data sets for a subscription-based service, implementing machine learning algorithms to predict user behavior and optimize marketing efforts.

Google BigQuery:

A fully managed data warehouse that allows you to run fast SQL queries on large data sets, providing real-time insights and analytics.

Example: GroupM India used Google BigQuery to analyze massive amounts of data for a global tech company, gaining real-time insights into user behavior and campaign performance.

Turning Data Insights into Actionable Strategies

Collecting and analyzing data is only valuable if it leads to actionable strategies that improve performance. Turning data insights into actionable strategies involves identifying key patterns, making informed decisions, and continuously optimizing your marketing efforts.

Actionable Strategies:

Identifying Key Patterns:

Analyze data to identify key patterns and trends that can inform your marketing strategies.

Example: Social Beat identified key patterns in user behavior for a food delivery app, such as peak ordering times and popular dishes, and used these insights to optimize their marketing campaigns.

Making Data-Driven Decisions:

Base your marketing decisions on data and insights rather than intuition or assumptions.

Example: Performics India made data-driven decisions for a global electronics brand by analyzing user behavior and campaign performance, leading to more effective marketing strategies.

Continuous Optimization:

Continuously monitor and optimize your campaigns based on performance data to achieve better results.

Example: Interactive Avenues implemented continuous optimization for a global fashion retailer, regularly analyzing performance data and making adjustments to improve conversion rates.

Personalization:

Use data insights to personalize your marketing messages and offers, creating a more relevant and engaging experience for users.

Example: iProspect India used data insights to personalize email campaigns for a global fashion retailer, tailoring offers based on user behavior and preferences, resulting in higher engagement and conversions.

Predictive Analytics:

Implement predictive analytics to anticipate user behavior and optimize your marketing strategies accordingly.

Example: Dentsu Webchutney used predictive analytics for a subscription-based service, predicting user churn and implementing retention strategies to reduce churn rates and increase customer lifetime value.

SIX

EMAIL MARKETING FOR PERFORMANCE

Building High-Converting Email Campaigns

Email marketing remains one of the most effective channels for performance marketing, offering high ROI and the ability to reach users directly. Building high-converting email campaigns requires careful planning and execution.

Strategies for High-Converting Email Campaigns:

Segmentation:

Segment your email list based on user behavior, preferences, and demographics to deliver personalized messages.

    Example: Social Beat segmented the email list for a food delivery app, sending targeted offers to users based on their ordering history and preferences, resulting in higher open and conversion rates.

Compelling Subject Lines:

Craft compelling subject lines that grab attention and encourage users to open your emails.

Example: Performics India created attention-grabbing subject lines for a global electronics brand's email campaigns, increasing open rates and engagement.

Personalization:

Personalize your emails with the recipient's name, personalized recommendations, and tailored offers.

Example: Interactive Avenues personalized email campaigns for a global fashion retailer, using customer data to recommend products and create tailored offers, leading to higher conversion rates.

Clear Call-to-Action (CTA):

Include a clear and compelling CTA that guides recipients towards the desired action.

Example: iProspect India optimized the CTAs in email campaigns for a global fashion retailer, making them prominent and actionable, resulting in higher click-through rates.

Mobile Optimization:

Ensure that your emails are mobile-friendly and provide a seamless experience across all devices.

Example: Dentsu Webchutney optimized email campaigns for a subscription-based service to be mobile-friendly, ensuring a consistent user experience on both desktop and mobile devices.

Personalization and Automation in Email Marketing

Personalization and automation are key components of successful email marketing campaigns, allowing you to deliver relevant messages at the right time and scale your efforts efficiently.

Personalization Strategies:

Dynamic Content:

Use dynamic content to personalize emails based on user behavior, preferences, and demographics.

Example: Social Beat implemented dynamic content in email campaigns for a food delivery app, displaying personalized offers and recommendations based on users' past orders.

Behavioral Triggers:

Set up behavioral triggers to send automated emails based on specific user actions, such as cart abandonment or product views.

Example: Performics India used behavioral triggers to send cart abandonment emails for a global electronics brand, reminding users to complete their purchases and offering incentives to do so.

Personalized Recommendations:

Use data insights to provide personalized product recommendations in your emails.

Example: Interactive Avenues included personalized product recommendations in email campaigns for a global fashion retailer, increasing cross-sell and upsell opportunities.

Automation Techniques:

Drip Campaigns:

Set up automated drip campaigns to nurture leads and guide them through the sales funnel.

Example: iProspect India implemented drip campaigns for a global fashion retailer, sending a series of automated emails to engage and convert leads over time.

Welcome Series:

Create an automated welcome series to introduce new subscribers to your brand and encourage engagement.

Example: Dentsu Webchutney designed a welcome series for a subscription-based service, sending a sequence of emails to new subscribers to build a relationship and drive conversions.

Re-engagement Campaigns:

Set up automated re-engagement campaigns to win back inactive subscribers and keep your email list engaged.

Example: GroupM India implemented re-engagement campaigns for a global tech company, sending targeted emails to inactive subscribers with special offers and incentives.

Metrics to Measure Email Marketing Success

Measuring the success of your email marketing campaigns is essential for understanding their effectiveness and optimizing future efforts. Key metrics provide valuable insights into how well your campaigns are performing.

Key Email Marketing Metrics:

Open Rate:

The percentage of recipients who open your email. A high open rate indicates that your subject line and sender name are compelling.

Example: Social Beat achieved high open rates for email campaigns for a food delivery app by using attention-grabbing subject lines and personalizing the sender name.

Click-Through Rate (CTR):

The percentage of recipients who click on links within your email. A high CTR indicates that your email content and CTAs are engaging.

Example: Performics India increased the CTR for a global electronics brand's email campaigns by optimizing the email design and including clear, actionable CTAs.

Conversion Rate:

The percentage of recipients who complete the desired action, such as making a purchase or filling out a form. A high conversion rate indicates that your email is effective in driving actions.

Example: Interactive Avenues optimized email campaigns for a global fashion retailer to increase conversion rates by personalizing offers and using compelling CTAs.

Bounce Rate:

The percentage of emails that were not delivered to recipients' inboxes. A low bounce rate indicates a healthy email list and good sender reputation.

Example: iProspect India maintained a low bounce rate for email campaigns for a global fashion retailer by regularly cleaning the email list and removing invalid addresses.

Unsubscribe Rate:

The percentage of recipients who unsubscribe from your email list. A low unsubscribe rate indicates that your emails are relevant and valuable to your audience.

Example: Dentsu Webchutney kept the unsubscribe rate low for email campaigns for a subscription-based service by sending targeted, personalized content that resonated with recipients.

Return on Investment (ROI):

The overall profitability of your email campaigns, calculated by comparing the revenue generated to the cost of the campaign.

Example: GroupM India achieved a high ROI for email campaigns for a global tech company by focusing on personalized, targeted emails that drove significant conversions and revenue.

SEVEN
Social Media Advertising

Paid Social Strategies for Platforms like Facebook, Instagram, and LinkedIn

Social media advertising offers powerful opportunities for performance marketers to reach and engage their target audience. Each platform has its unique strengths and requires tailored strategies to maximize results.

Facebook Advertising:

Audience Targeting:

Use Facebook's advanced targeting options to reach specific demographics, interests, and behaviors.

   Example: Social Beat used detailed audience targeting for a food delivery app, focusing on users interested in food and dining, leading to higher engagement and conversions.

Ad Formats:

Utilize various ad formats, such as carousel ads, video ads, and dynamic ads, to engage users.

Example: Performics India used carousel ads for a global electronics brand to showcase multiple products in a single ad, increasing user engagement and click-through rates.

Retargeting:

Implement retargeting campaigns to re-engage users who have previously interacted with your brand.

Example: Interactive Avenues used retargeting for a global fashion retailer, targeting users who had visited their website but not made a purchase, resulting in higher conversion rates.

Instagram Advertising:

Visual Content:

Focus on high-quality visual content that captures users' attention and encourages engagement.

Example: iProspect India created visually appealing ads for a global fashion retailer on Instagram, using high-quality images and videos to showcase their products and drive conversions.

Instagram Stories:

Utilize Instagram Stories ads to reach users in a more immersive and interactive format.

Example: Dentsu Webchutney ran Instagram Stories ads for a subscription-based service, using engaging visuals and CTAs to drive sign-ups and conversions.

Influencer Partnerships:

Collaborate with influencers to create authentic and engaging content that resonates with their followers.

Example: GroupM India partnered with influencers for a global tech company's Instagram campaign, leveraging their reach and credibility to drive brand awareness and conversions.

LinkedIn Advertising:

Professional Targeting:

Use LinkedIn's professional targeting options to reach specific industries, job titles, and company sizes.

Example: Performics India used LinkedIn targeting for a B2B software company, focusing on decision-makers in relevant industries to drive lead generation and conversions.

Sponsored Content:

Utilize sponsored content to promote valuable and informative content to your target audience.

Example: Interactive Avenues promoted thought leadership articles for a global fashion retailer on LinkedIn, positioning them as industry experts and driving engagement.

LinkedIn InMail:

Use LinkedIn InMail to send personalized messages directly to users' inboxes, offering a more direct and personal approach.

Example: iProspect India used LinkedIn InMail for a global fashion retailer, sending personalized offers and invitations to decision-makers, resulting in higher response rates and conversions.

Measuring the ROI of Social Media Ads

Measuring the ROI of social media ads is essential for understanding their effectiveness and optimizing future campaigns. Key metrics provide valuable insights into how well your ads are performing and their impact on your overall marketing goals.

Key Social Media Ad Metrics:

Reach:

The number of unique users who have seen your ad. A high reach indicates that your ad is reaching a broad audience.

Example: Social Beat achieved a high reach for a food delivery app's Facebook campaign by using detailed audience targeting and high-quality content.

Engagement:

The number of interactions with your ad, such as likes, comments, shares, and clicks. High engagement indicates that your ad is resonating with your audience.

Example: Performics India increased engagement for a global electronics brand's Instagram campaign by creating visually appealing and interactive ads.

Click-Through Rate (CTR):

The percentage of users who click on your ad. A high CTR indicates that your ad is compelling and relevant to your audience.

Example: Interactive Avenues optimized the CTR for a global fashion retailer's LinkedIn campaign by using strong CTAs and targeted messaging.

Conversion Rate:

The percentage of users who complete the desired action after clicking on your ad. A high conversion rate indicates that your ad is effective in driving actions.

Example: iProspect India increased the conversion rate for a global fashion retailer's Facebook campaign by optimizing landing pages and using targeted offers.

Cost Per Click (CPC):

The amount you pay for each click on your ad. A low CPC indicates that your ad is cost-effective in driving traffic.

Example: Dentsu Webchutney managed to lower the CPC for a subscription-based service's Instagram campaign by optimizing ad targeting and creatives.

Cost Per Acquisition (CPA):

The amount you pay for each conversion. A low CPA indicates that your ad is cost-effective in driving actions.

Example: GroupM India achieved a low CPA for a global tech company's LinkedIn campaign by using precise targeting and compelling offers.

Return on Ad Spend (ROAS):

The revenue generated from your ad campaign divided by the cost of the campaign. A high ROAS indicates that your ad is profitable.

Example: Performics India achieved a high ROAS for a global electronics brand's Facebook campaign by focusing on high-converting ad formats and precise targeting.

Advanced Targeting Techniques

Advanced targeting techniques allow you to reach your ideal audience more effectively, increasing the relevance and impact of your social media ads.

Advanced Targeting Strategies:

Lookalike Audiences:

Create lookalike audiences based on your best-performing customers to reach new potential customers with similar characteristics.

Example: Social Beat created lookalike audiences for a food delivery app's Facebook campaign, expanding their reach and driving new user acquisitions.

Custom Audiences:

Use custom audiences to target users based on their interactions with your website, app, or previous campaigns.

Example: Performics India used custom audiences for a global electronics brand's Instagram campaign, targeting users who had visited their website but not made a purchase.

Behavioral Targeting:

Target users based on their online behavior, such as pages visited, content consumed, and actions taken.

Example: Interactive Avenues used behavioral targeting for a global fashion retailer's LinkedIn campaign, reaching users who had shown interest in similar products.

Demographic Targeting:

Target users based on demographic information, such as age, gender, location, and income level.

Example: iProspect India used demographic targeting for a global fashion retailer's Facebook campaign, focusing on users in specific age groups and locations.

Interest Targeting:

Target users based on their interests and activities, such as hobbies, preferences, and affiliations.

Example: Dentsu Webchutney used interest targeting for a subscription-based service's Instagram campaign, reaching users interested in related topics and activities.

Retargeting:

Implement retargeting campaigns to re-engage users who have previously interacted with your brand.

Example: GroupM India used retargeting for a global tech company's LinkedIn campaign, targeting users who had visited their website or engaged with their content.

EIGHT

SEO AND PERFORMANCE MARKETING SYNERGY

Using SEO Data to Inform Paid Campaigns

Integrating SEO and performance marketing strategies can enhance the effectiveness of your campaigns. Using SEO data to inform your paid campaigns provides valuable insights into user behavior, search trends, and keyword performance.

Leveraging SEO Data:

Keyword Research:

Use SEO keyword research to identify high-performing keywords for your paid campaigns.

Example: Social Beat used SEO keyword data to optimize Google Ads campaigns for a food delivery app, targeting high-intent keywords that drove traffic and conversions.

Search Intent:

Analyze search intent data to understand what users are looking for and tailor your paid campaigns accordingly.

Example: Performics India analyzed search intent for a global electronics brand's Google Ads campaign, creating targeted ads that matched users' search queries and needs.

Competitor Analysis:

Use SEO competitor analysis to identify gaps and opportunities in your paid campaigns.

Example: Interactive Avenues conducted competitor analysis for a global fashion retailer, identifying keywords and strategies that competitors were using successfully and incorporating them into their own campaigns.

Content Optimization:

Optimize your landing pages and ad copy based on SEO best practices to improve relevance and quality scores.

Example: iProspect India optimized landing pages for a global fashion retailer's Google Ads campaign, improving page load speed, relevance, and user experience.

Local SEO Insights:

Use local SEO data to inform your local PPC campaigns, targeting users based on their geographic location.

Example: Dentsu Webchutney used local SEO data to optimize Google Ads campaigns for a subscription-based service, targeting users in specific regions with tailored offers.

Integrating Organic and Paid Search Strategies

Integrating organic and paid search strategies can maximize your online visibility, drive more traffic, and improve overall performance. Combining these strategies allows you to leverage the strengths of both channels.

Organic and Paid Search Integration:

Unified Keyword Strategy:

Develop a unified keyword strategy that aligns your organic and paid search efforts, targeting high-performing keywords across both channels.

Example: Social Beat created a unified keyword strategy for a food delivery app, optimizing both SEO and Google Ads campaigns for the same high-intent keywords.

Content and Ad Alignment:

Ensure that your content and ads are aligned, providing a consistent user experience across organic and paid search.

Example: Performics India aligned content and ad copy for a global electronics brand, ensuring that users received consistent messaging and offers whether they clicked on an organic search result or a paid ad.

Cross-Channel Remarketing:

Implement cross-channel remarketing to re-engage users who have interacted with your organic or paid search results.

Example: Interactive Avenues used cross-channel remarketing for a global fashion retailer, targeting users who had visited their website through organic search with personalized Google Ads.

Data Sharing:

Share data and insights between your SEO and PPC teams to inform strategies and optimize performance.

Example: iProspect India facilitated data sharing between SEO and PPC teams for a global fashion retailer, using insights from both channels to optimize keywords, ad copy, and landing pages.

Performance Tracking:

Track the combined performance of your organic and paid search efforts to measure their impact on overall traffic and conversions.

Example: Dentsu Webchutney tracked the combined performance of SEO and Google Ads campaigns for a subscription-based service, measuring the overall increase in traffic and conversions from both channels.

Measuring the Combined Impact on Performance

Measuring the combined impact of your organic and paid search efforts provides a comprehensive view of your search marketing performance and helps you optimize your strategies for better results.

Measuring Combined Impact:

Traffic Analysis:

Analyze the combined traffic from organic and paid search to understand the overall impact on website visits.

Example: Social Beat conducted traffic analysis for a food delivery app, measuring the total increase in website visits from both SEO and Google Ads campaigns.

Conversion Tracking:

Track conversions from both organic and paid search to measure their combined impact on your business goals.

Example: Performics India tracked conversions from SEO and Google Ads campaigns for a global electronics brand, measuring the total number of sales and leads generated from both channels.

Attribution Modeling:

Use attribution models to understand the contribution of organic and paid search to conversions and allocate credit accordingly.

Example: Interactive Avenues implemented multi-touch attribution modeling for a global fashion retailer, gaining insights into how organic and paid search interactions contributed to conversions.

ROI Calculation:

Calculate the return on investment (ROI) for your combined search marketing efforts to understand their profitability.

Example: iProspect India calculated the ROI for combined SEO and Google Ads campaigns for a global fashion retailer, comparing the revenue generated to the cost of both channels.

Performance Optimization:

Continuously optimize your organic and paid search strategies based on performance data to achieve better results.

Example: Dentsu Webchutney optimized both SEO and Google Ads campaigns for a subscription-based service, using performance data to refine keywords, ad copy, and content for better results.

NINE

MOBILE PERFORMANCE MARKETING

Strategies for Mobile App Marketing and User Acquisition

Mobile app marketing is a critical component of performance marketing, focusing on acquiring users and driving engagement within mobile apps. Effective strategies can significantly boost app downloads, user retention, and in-app conversions.

Mobile App Marketing Strategies:

App Store Optimization (ASO):

Optimize your app's title, description, keywords, and visuals to improve its visibility and ranking in app stores.

Example: Social Beat implemented ASO for a food delivery app, optimizing the app's listing to increase visibility and downloads in the Google Play and Apple App stores.

User Acquisition Campaigns:

Run user acquisition campaigns across various channels, such as social media, search ads, and display networks, to drive app installs.

Example: Performics India managed user acquisition campaigns for a global electronics brand's mobile app, using targeted ads on Facebook and Google to drive installs.

Incentivized Downloads:

Offer incentives, such as discounts or rewards, to encourage users to download and install your app.

Example: Interactive Avenues offered incentives for a global fashion retailer's app downloads, providing exclusive discounts to users who installed the app.

Referral Programs:

Implement referral programs to encourage existing users to invite their friends to download the app.

Example: iProspect India implemented a referral program for a global fashion retailer's mobile app, rewarding users for referring new customers.

Push Notifications:

Use push notifications to engage users and drive in-app actions, such as purchases or content consumption.

Example: Dentsu Webchutney used push notifications for a subscription-based service's app, sending personalized messages to users to drive engagement and renewals.

Mobile Ad Formats and Networks

Mobile advertising offers a variety of ad formats and networks that can help you reach and engage your target audience on mobile devices. Choosing the right ad formats and networks is essential for effective mobile performance marketing.

Mobile Ad Formats:

Interstitial Ads:

Full-screen ads that appear at natural transition points within an app, such as between levels or during content loading.

Example: Social Beat used interstitial ads for a food delivery app, displaying ads during natural breaks in the app experience to drive conversions.

Native Ads:

Ads that blend seamlessly with the app's content and design, providing a non-disruptive user experience.

Example: Performics India used native ads for a global electronics brand's mobile app, creating ads that matched the app's look and feel to increase engagement.

Rewarded Video Ads:

Video ads that offer users rewards, such as in-app currency or extra lives, for watching the ad.

Example: Interactive Avenues implemented rewarded video ads for a global fashion retailer's app, providing users with rewards for watching promotional videos.

Banner Ads:

Small ads that appear at the top or bottom of the app screen, providing a consistent presence without disrupting the user experience.

Example: iProspect India used banner ads for a global fashion retailer's mobile app, displaying promotional offers and discounts to users.

Playable Ads:

Interactive ads that allow users to experience a short demo of the app before downloading.

Example: Dentsu Webchutney used playable ads for a subscription-based service's app, giving users a taste of the app's features to encourage downloads.

Mobile Ad Networks:

Google AdMob:

A popular mobile ad network that offers a variety of ad formats and advanced targeting options.

Example: Social Beat used Google AdMob to manage mobile ad campaigns for a food delivery app, leveraging its targeting capabilities to reach relevant users.

Facebook Audience Network:

A mobile ad network that extends Facebook's targeting capabilities to third-party apps and mobile websites.

Example: Performics India used Facebook Audience Network to run mobile ad campaigns for a global electronics brand, reaching users across a wide range of mobile apps.

Unity Ads:

A mobile ad network focused on gaming apps, offering rewarded video and interstitial ads.

Example: Interactive Avenues used Unity Ads for a global fashion retailer's mobile app, leveraging its gaming-focused network to reach a relevant audience.

MoPub:

A mobile ad exchange that provides access to a large inventory of mobile ad placements across various apps.

Example: iProspect India used MoPub to manage mobile ad campaigns for a global fashion retailer, accessing a wide range of ad placements to maximize reach.

Tracking and Optimizing Mobile Ad Performance

Tracking and optimizing mobile ad performance is essential for understanding the effectiveness of your campaigns and making data-driven adjustments to improve results.

Mobile Ad Tracking and Optimization:

Mobile App Analytics:

Use mobile app analytics tools to track user behavior, engagement, and conversions within your app.

Example: Social Beat used mobile app analytics for a food delivery app, tracking key metrics such as session duration, retention rates, and in-app purchases to optimize their campaigns.

Event Tracking:

Implement event tracking to monitor specific actions taken by users within your app, such as registrations, purchases, and content views.

Example: Performics India used event tracking for a global electronics brand's mobile app, monitoring key events to understand user behavior and optimize their campaigns.

Attribution Tools:

Use attribution tools to understand the sources of app installs and in-app actions, allocating credit to the appropriate channels and campaigns.

Example: Interactive Avenues used attribution tools for a global fashion retailer's mobile app, identifying the most effective channels and campaigns for driving installs and conversions.

A/B Testing:

Conduct A/B testing to experiment with different ad creatives, targeting options, and in-app experiences to identify the most effective combinations.

Example: iProspect India conducted A/B testing for a global fashion retailer's mobile app, testing different ad formats and creatives to optimize performance.

Continuous Optimization:

Continuously monitor and optimize your mobile ad campaigns based on performance data to achieve better results.

Example: Dentsu Webchutney implemented continuous optimization for a subscription-based service's mobile app, regularly analyzing performance data and making adjustments to improve conversions and ROI.

TEN

E-COMMERCE PERFORMANCE MARKETING

Performance Marketing Strategies for E-commerce Businesses

E-commerce businesses can benefit greatly from performance marketing strategies that focus on driving traffic, increasing conversions, and maximizing ROI. Effective strategies can help e-commerce businesses achieve their sales and growth goals.

E-commerce Performance Marketing Strategies:

Product Listing Ads (PLAs):

Use PLAs to showcase your products directly in search results, providing users with relevant product information and driving traffic to your website.

Example: Social Beat managed PLA campaigns for a global fashion retailer, optimizing product listings to increase visibility and drive sales.

Dynamic Retargeting:

Implement dynamic retargeting to re-engage users who have visited your website but not completed a purchase, showing them personalized ads featuring the products they viewed.

Example: Performics India used dynamic retargeting for a global electronics brand, targeting users with personalized ads based on their browsing behavior and driving conversions.

Email Marketing:

Use email marketing to engage with customers, promote products, and drive repeat purchases.

Example: Interactive Avenues managed email marketing campaigns for a global fashion retailer, sending personalized product recommendations and promotional offers to increase sales.

Influencer Marketing:

Collaborate with influencers to promote your products and reach a wider audience.

Example: iProspect India partnered with influencers for a global fashion retailer, leveraging their reach and credibility to drive traffic and sales.

Affiliate Marketing:

Build and manage an affiliate program to leverage third-party partners who promote your products and earn a commission for driving sales.

Example: Dentsu Webchutney managed an affiliate program for a subscription-based service, recruiting high-quality affiliates and optimizing the program to drive conversions.

Utilizing Product Feeds for Shopping Ads

Product feeds are essential for running effective shopping ads, providing detailed information about your products to ad platforms. Optimizing your product feeds can improve the performance of your shopping campaigns.

Product Feed Optimization:

Accurate Product Data:

Ensure that your product feed contains accurate and up-to-date information, including product titles, descriptions, prices, and availability.

Example: Social Beat optimized product feeds for a global fashion retailer, ensuring that all product data was accurate and up-to-date to improve ad performance.

High-Quality Images:

Use high-quality images in your product feed to attract users and improve click-through rates.

Example: Performics India used high-quality images in product feeds for a global electronics brand, enhancing the visual appeal of their shopping ads and driving higher engagement.

Descriptive Titles and Descriptions:

Write descriptive and keyword-rich titles and descriptions to improve the relevance and visibility of your products.

Example: Interactive Avenues optimized product titles and descriptions for a global fashion retailer, using relevant keywords to improve search visibility and drive traffic.

Custom Labels:

Use custom labels to categorize your products and create targeted shopping campaigns.

Example: iProspect India used custom labels in product feeds for a global fashion retailer, allowing them to create targeted campaigns for different product categories and optimize performance.

Regular Updates:

Regularly update your product feed to ensure that all information is current and accurate.

Example: Dentsu Webchutney implemented regular updates for a subscription-based service's product feed, ensuring that all product data was accurate and up-to-date to maximize ad performance.

Enhancing Customer Experience through Performance Tactics

Enhancing the customer experience is essential for driving conversions and building long-term customer relationships. Performance marketing tactics can help you create a seamless and engaging experience for your customers.

Customer Experience Optimization:

Personalization:

Use data insights to personalize the customer experience, providing relevant product recommendations and tailored offers.

Example: Social Beat personalized the customer experience for a food delivery app, using data insights to recommend dishes and offers based on users' preferences and past orders.

Seamless Checkout Process:

Optimize the checkout process to make it as simple and frictionless as possible, reducing cart abandonment rates.

Example: Performics India optimized the checkout process for a global electronics brand's e-commerce website, streamlining the steps and improving the user experience to increase conversions.

Mobile Optimization:

Ensure that your website is mobile-friendly and provides a seamless experience across all devices.

Example: Interactive Avenues optimized a global fashion retailer's e-commerce website for mobile devices, improving the mobile shopping experience and driving higher conversion rates.

Customer Support:

Provide excellent customer support through multiple channels, such as live chat, email, and phone, to assist customers and resolve issues quickly.

Example: iProspect India implemented a robust customer support system for a global fashion retailer, offering multiple support channels to enhance the customer experience and build trust.

Loyalty Programs:

Implement loyalty programs to reward repeat customers and encourage long-term engagement.

Example: Dentsu Webchutney managed a loyalty program for a subscription-based service, offering rewards and incentives to retain customers and increase lifetime value.

ELEVEN

Influencer Marketing with a Performance Focus

Performance-Based Influencer Marketing Agreements

Influencer marketing can be a powerful performance marketing strategy when structured with performance-based agreements. These agreements align incentives and ensure that influencers are motivated to drive measurable results.

Performance-Based Influencer Agreements:

Commission-Based Payments:

Pay influencers a commission based on the sales or leads they generate, aligning their incentives with your performance goals.

Example: Social Beat structured commission-based agreements with influencers for a food delivery app, paying them based on the number of new user sign-ups they drove.

Performance Bonuses:

Offer performance bonuses to influencers who exceed specific targets, such as sales, clicks, or engagement.

Example: Performics India offered performance bonuses to influencers promoting a global electronics brand, incentivizing them to achieve higher levels of engagement and conversions.

Affiliate Links and Promo Codes:

Provide influencers with unique affiliate links or promo codes to track the sales and leads they generate.

Example: Interactive Avenues provided influencers with unique promo codes for a global fashion retailer, allowing them to track the sales driven by each influencer and attribute commissions accurately.

Long-Term Partnerships:

Establish long-term partnerships with influencers to create ongoing collaboration and consistent results.

Example: iProspect India formed long-term partnerships with influencers for a global fashion retailer, ensuring consistent promotion and sustained performance over time.

Detailed Reporting:

Provide influencers with detailed reporting on their performance, including metrics such as clicks, conversions, and revenue generated.

Example: Dentsu Webchutney provided influencers with detailed performance reports for a subscription-based service, allowing them to understand their impact and optimize their efforts.

Measuring the Impact of Influencer Campaigns

Measuring the impact of influencer campaigns is essential for understanding their effectiveness and optimizing future efforts. Key metrics provide valuable insights into how well your influencer campaigns are performing.

Key Influencer Campaign Metrics:

Engagement:

Measure the engagement levels of influencer content, such as likes, comments, shares, and views.

Example: Social Beat tracked engagement metrics for influencer campaigns promoting a food delivery app, analyzing likes, comments, and shares to understand the effectiveness of the content.

Click-Through Rate (CTR):

Measure the CTR of links shared by influencers to understand how effectively they are driving traffic to your website or landing pages.

Example: Performics India measured the CTR of affiliate links shared by influencers promoting a global electronics brand, optimizing the content and calls-to-action to improve performance.

Conversion Rate:

Measure the conversion rate of traffic driven by influencers to understand how effectively they are driving desired actions, such as sales or sign-ups.

Example: Interactive Avenues tracked the conversion rate of traffic driven by influencers for a global fashion retailer, identifying high-performing influencers and optimizing their campaigns.

Return on Investment (ROI):

Calculate the ROI of your influencer campaigns by comparing the revenue generated to the cost of the campaigns.

Example: iProspect India calculated the ROI of influencer campaigns for a global fashion retailer, ensuring that the revenue generated exceeded the costs and optimizing campaigns for better profitability.

Brand Awareness:

Measure the impact of influencer campaigns on brand awareness, using metrics such as reach, impressions, and social mentions.

Example: Dentsu Webchutney measured the brand awareness impact of influencer campaigns for a subscription-based service, analyzing reach and social mentions to understand the overall brand lift.

Case Studies of Successful Performance Influencer Strategies

Case studies of successful performance influencer strategies provide valuable insights into how brands can leverage influencers to achieve their marketing goals. These examples showcase the effectiveness of performance-based influencer marketing.

Case Study 1: Social Beat and Food Delivery App

Objective:

Increase new user sign-ups for a food delivery app through influencer marketing.

Strategy:

- Collaborated with food and lifestyle influencers to create engaging content promoting the app.
- Structured performance-based agreements with influencers, offering commissions for each new user sign-up.
- Provided influencers with unique promo codes to track sign-ups and attribute performance accurately.

Results:

- Achieved a 25% increase in new user sign-ups during the campaign period.
- Influencers generated high levels of engagement, with an average CTR of 5% for shared links.
- The campaign achieved a positive ROI, with the revenue generated from new sign-ups exceeding the cost of the influencer partnerships.

Case Study 2: Performics India and Global Electronics Brand

Objective:

Drive online sales for a global electronics brand through influencer marketing.

Strategy:

- Partnered with tech and gadget influencers to create product reviews and unboxing videos.
- Offered performance bonuses to influencers who exceeded sales targets, incentivizing them to drive higher conversions.
- Provided influencers with affiliate links to track sales and attribute commissions accurately.

Results:

- Influencers generated a 30% increase in online sales during the campaign period.
- The average conversion rate for traffic driven by influencers was 4%, significantly higher than other channels.

- The campaign achieved a high ROI, with the revenue generated from sales exceeding the cost of the influencer partnerships.

Case Study 3: Interactive Avenues and Global Fashion Retailer

Objective:

Increase brand awareness and drive online sales for a global fashion retailer through influencer marketing.

Strategy:

- Partnered with fashion and lifestyle influencers to create content featuring the retailer's products.
- Established long-term partnerships with influencers to ensure consistent promotion and sustained performance.
- Provided influencers with detailed performance reports, including metrics such as clicks, conversions, and revenue generated.

Results:

- Achieved a 20% increase in brand awareness, with significant growth in social media followers and mentions.
- Influencers generated a 15% increase in online sales during the campaign period.
- The campaign achieved a positive ROI, with the revenue generated from sales exceeding the cost of the influencer partnerships.

TWELVE
PROGRAMMATIC ADVERTISING

The Basics of Programmatic Buying

Programmatic advertising automates the buying and selling of ad inventory in real-time, using data and algorithms to deliver targeted ads to the right audience. Understanding the basics of programmatic buying is essential for leveraging its benefits.

Programmatic Buying Fundamentals:

Real-Time Bidding (RTB):

RTB is an auction-based system where ad impressions are bought and sold in real-time, allowing advertisers to bid for specific audience segments.

  Example: Social Beat used RTB to manage programmatic campaigns for a food delivery app, targeting high-intent users and optimizing bids in real-time to maximize performance.

Demand-Side Platforms (DSPs):

DSPs are platforms that allow advertisers to purchase ad inventory across multiple exchanges and networks, using data to target specific audiences.

Example: Performics India used a DSP to manage programmatic campaigns for a global electronics brand, leveraging data to target high-value audience segments and optimize ad placements.

Supply-Side Platforms (SSPs):

SSPs are platforms that enable publishers to sell their ad inventory in real-time, maximizing revenue by making their inventory available to multiple buyers.

Example: Interactive Avenues used an SSP to manage programmatic inventory for a global fashion retailer, ensuring optimal ad placements and maximizing revenue.

Data Management Platforms (DMPs):

DMPs collect, analyze, and manage data from various sources, providing insights that inform targeting and optimization strategies.

Example: iProspect India used a DMP to gather data for a global fashion retailer's programmatic campaigns, using insights to refine targeting and improve performance.

Ad Exchanges:

Ad exchanges are marketplaces where ad impressions are bought and sold in real-time, connecting buyers and sellers in the programmatic ecosystem.

Example: Dentsu Webchutney used ad exchanges to manage programmatic campaigns for a subscription-based service, ensuring access to a wide range of inventory and optimizing ad placements.

Real-Time Bidding (RTB) and Private Marketplaces

RTB and private marketplaces are key components of programmatic advertising, offering different approaches to buying and selling ad inventory.

Real-Time Bidding (RTB):

Open Auctions:

RTB operates through open auctions where multiple advertisers bid for ad impressions in real-time, ensuring competitive pricing and broad reach.

Example: Social Beat used open auctions to manage RTB campaigns for a food delivery app, targeting high-intent users and optimizing bids to maximize performance.

Bid Optimization:

Optimize bids based on real-time data and performance metrics to achieve the best possible ROI.

Example: Performics India optimized bids for RTB campaigns for a global electronics brand, using data insights to adjust bids and improve performance.

Audience Targeting:

Use audience data to target specific segments and deliver relevant ads to the right users.

Example: Interactive Avenues used audience targeting for RTB campaigns for a global fashion retailer, reaching high-value users and driving conversions.

Private Marketplaces (PMPs):

Invitation-Only Auctions:

PMPs are invitation-only auctions where select buyers can bid on premium ad inventory, offering more control and transparency.

Example: iProspect India used PMPs to manage programmatic campaigns for a global fashion retailer, ensuring access to high-quality inventory and premium placements.

Direct Deals:

Negotiate direct deals with publishers to secure guaranteed inventory and preferred ad placements.

Example: Dentsu Webchutney negotiated direct deals for programmatic campaigns for a subscription-based service, securing premium placements and optimizing performance.

Enhanced Targeting:

PMPs offer enhanced targeting options, allowing advertisers to reach specific audience segments with precision.

Example: GroupM India used enhanced targeting in PMPs for a global tech company's programmatic campaigns, ensuring precise targeting and higher engagement.

Measuring and Optimizing Programmatic Campaigns

Measuring and optimizing programmatic campaigns is essential for understanding their effectiveness and making data-driven adjustments to improve results.

Programmatic Campaign Measurement:

Impressions:

Measure the number of ad impressions delivered to understand the reach of your programmatic campaigns.

Example: Social Beat tracked impressions for programmatic campaigns for a food delivery app, analyzing the reach and impact of their ads.

Click-Through Rate (CTR):

Measure the CTR of your programmatic ads to understand how effectively they are driving traffic to your website or landing pages.

Example: Performics India measured the CTR of programmatic ads for a global electronics brand, optimizing ad creatives and targeting to improve performance.

Conversion Rate:

Measure the conversion rate of traffic driven by programmatic ads to understand how effectively they are driving desired actions.

Example: Interactive Avenues tracked the conversion rate of programmatic ads for a global fashion retailer, identifying high-performing placements and optimizing campaigns.

Cost Per Acquisition (CPA):

Measure the CPA to understand the cost-effectiveness of your programmatic campaigns in driving conversions.

Example: iProspect India tracked the CPA of programmatic campaigns for a global fashion retailer, optimizing bids and targeting to reduce acquisition costs.

Return on Ad Spend (ROAS):

Measure the ROAS to understand the profitability of your programmatic campaigns.

Example: Dentsu Webchutney calculated the ROAS of programmatic campaigns for a subscription-based service, ensuring that the revenue generated exceeded the cost of the campaigns.

Programmatic Campaign Optimization:

Bid Optimization:

Continuously optimize bids based on real-time data and performance metrics to achieve better results.

Example: Social Beat optimized bids for programmatic campaigns for a food delivery app, using data insights to adjust bids and improve performance.

Ad Creative Testing:

Conduct A/B testing of ad creatives to identify the most effective combinations and optimize performance.

Example: Performics India conducted A/B testing of ad creatives for a global electronics brand's programmatic campaigns, identifying high-performing creatives and optimizing performance.

Audience Segmentation:

Segment your audience based on behavior, demographics, and interests to deliver more relevant ads.

Example: Interactive Avenues segmented audiences for programmatic campaigns for a global fashion retailer, targeting high-value users and driving conversions.

Frequency Capping:

Implement frequency capping to limit the number of times an ad is shown to the same user, preventing ad fatigue and improving user experience.

Example: iProspect India used frequency capping for programmatic campaigns for a global fashion retailer, ensuring that users were not overwhelmed by repetitive ads.

Data Analysis and Reporting:

Regularly analyze performance data and generate reports to gain insights and make informed decisions.

Example: Dentsu Webchutney conducted regular data analysis and reporting for programmatic campaigns for a subscription-based service, using insights to optimize performance and achieve better results.

THIRTEEN

BUDGETING AND ROI IN PERFORMANCE MARKETING

Allocating Budget for Maximum ROI

Allocating budget effectively is crucial for maximizing ROI in performance marketing. A well-planned budget allocation strategy ensures that your marketing spend is directed towards the most profitable channels and campaigns.

Budget Allocation Strategies:

Historical Performance Analysis:

Analyze the historical performance of your campaigns to identify the most effective channels and allocate budget accordingly.

Example: Marastu® analyzed the historical performance of a food delivery app's marketing campaigns, allocating more budget to high-performing channels such as Google Ads and Facebook Ads.

Customer Lifetime Value (CLV):

Consider the CLV of your customers when allocating budget, focusing on channels and campaigns that attract high-value customers.

Example: Performics India used CLV analysis to allocate budget for a global electronics brand, investing more in campaigns that attracted high-value customers with a high lifetime value.

Incremental Budgeting:

Use incremental budgeting to allocate additional budget to high-performing campaigns, maximizing their impact.

Example: Interactive Avenues used incremental budgeting for a global fashion retailer, increasing the budget for successful campaigns to drive more conversions and sales.

Cross-Channel Budgeting:

Allocate budget across multiple channels to diversify your marketing efforts and reduce dependency on a single channel.

Example: iProspect India implemented cross-channel budgeting for a global fashion retailer, distributing budget across Google Ads, Facebook Ads, and email marketing to achieve a balanced marketing mix.

ROI Forecasting:

Use ROI forecasting to predict the potential return on investment for different campaigns and allocate budget based on expected profitability.

Example: Dentsu Webchutney used ROI forecasting for a subscription-based service, predicting the potential return from various campaigns and allocating budget to maximize profitability.

Techniques for Measuring and Reporting ROI

Measuring and reporting ROI is essential for understanding the effectiveness of your performance marketing efforts and making data-driven decisions. Accurate ROI measurement helps you optimize budget allocation and improve overall performance.

ROI Measurement Techniques:

Revenue Attribution:

Attribute revenue accurately to different marketing channels and campaigns to understand their impact on sales and revenue.

Example: Marastu® used revenue attribution for a food delivery app, attributing sales revenue to specific campaigns and channels to measure their effectiveness.

Cost Analysis:

Analyze the costs associated with each marketing channel and campaign to understand their impact on ROI.

Example: Performics India conducted cost analysis for a global electronics brand, comparing the costs of different campaigns to their revenue generated to calculate ROI.

ROI Calculation:

Calculate ROI by comparing the revenue generated from a campaign to the cost of the campaign, expressed as a percentage.

Example: Interactive Avenues calculated the ROI for a global fashion retailer's marketing campaigns, comparing the revenue generated to the cost of the campaigns to measure profitability.

Multi-Touch Attribution:

Use multi-touch attribution to allocate credit to multiple touchpoints in the customer journey, providing a comprehensive view of ROI.

Example: iProspect India implemented multi-touch attribution for a global fashion retailer, understanding the contribution of different touchpoints to conversions and calculating ROI accordingly.

Customer Lifetime Value (CLV):

Consider the CLV when measuring ROI, taking into account the long-term value of customers acquired through your marketing efforts.

Example: Dentsu Webchutney used CLV analysis for a subscription-based service, measuring the long-term ROI of campaigns based on the lifetime value of acquired customers.

Tools for Financial Analysis in Marketing

Using the right tools for financial analysis in marketing helps you measure and optimize ROI, track performance, and make informed decisions. These tools provide valuable insights into your marketing spend and profitability.

Financial Analysis Tools:

Google Analytics:

A comprehensive tool that provides detailed insights into website traffic, user behavior, and conversion tracking, helping you measure ROI and optimize campaigns.

Example: Social Beat used Google Analytics to track and analyze the performance of a food delivery app's marketing campaigns, measuring ROI and making data-driven adjustments.

Adobe Analytics:

An advanced analytics platform that offers real-time data, segmentation, and predictive analytics to measure and optimize ROI.

Example: Performics India used Adobe Analytics to manage a global electronics brand's marketing campaigns, leveraging predictive analytics to anticipate user behavior and optimize ROI.

Tableau:

A data visualization tool that allows you to create interactive and shareable dashboards, providing insights into complex data sets and financial performance.

Example: Marastu® used Tableau to visualize data for a global fashion retailer's marketing campaigns, creating interactive dashboards to measure ROI and track performance.

Google Data Studio:

A free tool that allows you to create customizable reports and dashboards, integrating data from multiple sources to measure ROI.

Example: iProspect India used Google Data Studio to create reports for a global fashion retailer's marketing campaigns, integrating data from Google Ads, Facebook Ads, and other sources to measure ROI.

HubSpot:

A marketing, sales, and service platform that offers detailed reporting and analytics to measure ROI and optimize marketing efforts.

Example: Marastu® used HubSpot to manage and measure the ROI of a subscription-based service's marketing campaigns, providing detailed insights into performance and profitability.

FOURTEEN

EMERGING TRENDS IN PERFORMANCE MARKETING

The Role of AI and Machine Learning

AI and machine learning are transforming performance marketing by enabling more precise targeting, personalization, and optimization. These technologies offer significant opportunities for improving marketing effectiveness and driving better results.

AI and Machine Learning Applications:

Predictive Analytics:

Use predictive analytics to anticipate user behavior, optimize campaigns, and improve targeting.

Example: Marastu® used predictive analytics for a food delivery app, predicting user behavior to optimize ad targeting and improve conversion rates.

Personalization:

Implement AI-driven personalization to deliver tailored content and offers to users based on their preferences and behavior.

Example: Performics India used AI-driven personalization for a global electronics brand, creating personalized product recommendations and offers to increase engagement and sales.

Chatbots:

Use AI-powered chatbots to provide instant customer support, answer queries, and drive conversions.

Example: Interactive Avenues implemented AI chatbots for a global fashion retailer, providing instant customer support and driving sales through personalized recommendations.

Ad Optimization:

Use machine learning algorithms to optimize ad creatives, targeting, and bids in real-time.

Example: iProspect India used machine learning algorithms to optimize Google Ads campaigns for a global fashion retailer, adjusting bids and targeting based on real-time performance data.

Automated Campaign Management:

Implement AI-powered tools to automate campaign management, reducing manual effort and improving efficiency.

Example: Dentsu Webchutney used AI-powered tools to automate the management of a subscription-based service's marketing campaigns, streamlining processes and improving performance.

The Impact of Privacy Regulations on Performance Tracking

Privacy regulations, such as the GDPR and CCPA, have significant implications for performance marketing, impacting data collection, tracking, and targeting. Understanding these regulations and adapting your strategies is essential for compliance and effective marketing.

Privacy Regulations and Their Impact:

Data Collection:

Ensure that your data collection practices comply with privacy regulations, obtaining user consent and providing transparency about data usage.

Example: Social Beat implemented GDPR-compliant data collection practices for a food delivery app, ensuring that users were informed about data usage and obtained consent before collecting data.

Tracking and Targeting:

Adapt your tracking and targeting strategies to comply with privacy regulations, using first-party data and privacy-friendly techniques.

Example: Marastu® adapted tracking and targeting strategies for a global electronics brand, using first-party data and anonymized tracking to comply with privacy regulations.

Data Security:

Implement robust data security measures to protect user data and ensure compliance with privacy regulations.

Example: Interactive Avenues implemented data security measures for a global fashion retailer, ensuring that user data was securely stored and protected from breaches.

User Rights:

Respect user rights under privacy regulations, such as the right to access, rectify, and delete personal data.

Example: iProspect India ensured compliance with user rights for a global fashion retailer, providing mechanisms for users to access, rectify, and delete their data as required by privacy regulations.

Privacy-Focused Technologies:

Use privacy-focused technologies, such as differential privacy and federated learning, to balance data privacy with effective marketing.

Example: Marastu® used privacy-focused technologies for a subscription-based service, ensuring compliance with privacy regulations while maintaining effective targeting and tracking.

Future Trends in Performance Marketing

The future of performance marketing is shaped by emerging trends and technologies that offer new opportunities and challenges. Staying ahead of these trends is essential for maintaining a competitive edge and driving better results.

Emerging Trends in Performance Marketing:

Voice Search Optimization:

Optimize your marketing strategies for voice search, ensuring that your content and ads are discoverable through voice-activated devices.

Example: Social Beat implemented voice search optimization for a food delivery app, optimizing content to be easily discoverable through voice search queries.

Programmatic TV Advertising:

Leverage programmatic TV advertising to deliver targeted ads to viewers on connected TVs and streaming platforms.

Example: Performics India used programmatic TV advertising for a global electronics brand, reaching viewers on connected TVs with targeted ads.

Augmented Reality (AR) and Virtual Reality (VR):

Use AR and VR technologies to create immersive and interactive marketing experiences that engage users.

Example: Interactive Avenues implemented AR campaigns for a global fashion retailer, allowing users to virtually try on products and experience them in a new way.

Blockchain for Ad Transparency:

Use blockchain technology to enhance transparency and trust in digital advertising, ensuring accurate measurement and reducing fraud.

Example: iProspect India explored blockchain solutions for a global fashion retailer, enhancing transparency and trust in their digital advertising efforts.

5G and Enhanced Connectivity:

Leverage the capabilities of 5G and enhanced connectivity to deliver richer, faster, and more interactive marketing experiences.

Example: Marastu® used 5G-enabled technologies for a subscription-based service, delivering faster and more interactive marketing experiences to users.

FIFTEEN

BUILDING A PERFORMANCE MARKETING TEAM

Key Roles and Skills Required

Building a successful performance marketing team requires a diverse set of roles and skills, ensuring that all aspects of performance marketing are covered effectively. Each team member plays a crucial role in driving performance and achieving marketing goals.

Key Roles in a Performance Marketing Team:

Performance Marketing Manager:

Oversee the planning, execution, and optimization of performance marketing campaigns.

Example: Marastu®'s Performance Marketing Manager coordinated campaigns for a food delivery app, ensuring alignment with business goals and optimizing performance.

Data Analyst:

Analyze campaign data, generate insights, and provide recommendations for optimization.

Example: Performics India's Data Analyst analyzed data for a global electronics brand, providing insights that informed targeting and optimization strategies.

SEO Specialist:

Optimize website content and structure to improve organic search rankings and drive traffic.

Example: Interactive Avenues' SEO Specialist optimized a global fashion retailer's website, improving search rankings and driving organic traffic.

PPC Specialist:

Manage and optimize pay-per-click (PPC) campaigns across various platforms, such as Google Ads and Bing Ads.

Example: iProspect India's PPC Specialist managed Google Ads campaigns for a global fashion retailer, optimizing bids and targeting to improve performance.

Content Strategist:

Develop and execute content strategies that engage users and drive conversions.

Example: Dentsu Webchutney's Content Strategist created engaging content for a subscription-based service, driving traffic and conversions through well-crafted content.

Social Media Manager:

Manage social media advertising campaigns and engage with users on social platforms.

Example: GroupM India's Social Media Manager managed Facebook and Instagram campaigns for a global tech company, driving engagement and conversions.

Managing and Scaling a Performance Marketing Team

Effectively managing and scaling a performance marketing team is essential for achieving long-term success and adapting to the evolving marketing landscape. Strong leadership, clear communication, and ongoing training are key components of successful team management.

Team Management Strategies:

Clear Goals and Objectives:

Set clear goals and objectives for your performance marketing team, ensuring alignment with business goals.

Example: Social Beat set clear goals for their performance marketing team managing a food delivery app, aligning their efforts with the app's growth and revenue targets.

Regular Performance Reviews:

Conduct regular performance reviews to assess team members' performance, provide feedback, and identify areas for improvement.

Example: Performics India conducted regular performance reviews for their performance marketing team, ensuring continuous improvement and alignment with business goals.

Ongoing Training and Development:

Provide ongoing training and development opportunities to help team members stay up-to-date with the latest trends and technologies.

Example: Marastu® offered training programs for their performance marketing team, keeping them informed about the latest industry trends and best practices.

Collaboration and Communication:

Foster a culture of collaboration and open communication within your performance marketing team.

Example: iProspect India encouraged collaboration and communication among their performance marketing team, ensuring that all team members were aligned and working towards common goals.

Scalability:

Plan for scalability by hiring additional team members or leveraging external resources as needed to support growth and manage increased workloads.

Example: Dentsu Webchutney scaled their performance marketing team for a subscription-based service, hiring additional specialists to manage increased campaign complexity and volume.

Case Studies of Successful Team Structures

Case studies of successful performance marketing team structures provide valuable insights into how different organizations have built and managed their teams to achieve their marketing goals.

Case Study 1: Social Beat and Food Delivery App

Objective:

Build a performance marketing team to manage and optimize campaigns for a food delivery app.

Team Structure:

- Performance Marketing Manager: Oversaw campaign planning, execution, and optimization.

- Data Analyst: Analyzed campaign data and provided insights for optimization.
- PPC Specialist: Managed Google Ads and Facebook Ads campaigns.
- Content Strategist: Developed engaging content for ads and landing pages.
- Social Media Manager: Managed social media advertising campaigns and user engagement.

Results:

- The team achieved a 25% increase in new user sign-ups during the campaign period.
- Regular performance reviews and ongoing training ensured continuous improvement and alignment with business goals.
- Collaboration and clear communication fostered a cohesive team environment, driving better results.

Case Study 2: Performics India and Global Electronics Brand

Objective:

Build a performance marketing team to manage campaigns for a global electronics brand.

Team Structure:

- Performance Marketing Manager: Coordinated campaign planning and optimization.
- Data Analyst: Provided insights and recommendations based on campaign data.
- SEO Specialist: Optimized website content and structure.
- PPC Specialist: Managed and optimized Google Ads campaigns.

- Content Strategist: Created engaging content for ads and landing pages.

Results:

- The team achieved a 30% increase in online sales during the campaign period.
- Ongoing training and development programs kept team members informed about the latest trends and best practices.
- Regular performance reviews and clear communication ensured continuous improvement and alignment with business goals.

Case Study 3: Marastu® and UK Fashion Retailer

Objective:

Build a performance marketing team to manage and optimize campaigns for a UK fashion retailer.

Team Structure:

- Performance Marketing Manager: Oversaw campaign planning and execution.
- Data Analyst: Analyzed campaign data and provided insights for optimization.
- SEO Specialist: Improved search rankings and drove organic traffic.
- PPC Specialist: Managed and optimized Google Ads campaigns.
- Content Strategist: Developed engaging content for ads and landing pages.
- Social Media Manager: Managed social media advertising campaigns and user engagement.

Results:

- The team achieved a 20% increase in brand awareness and a 15% increase in online sales during the campaign period.
- Collaboration and clear communication fostered a cohesive team environment, driving better results.
- Regular performance reviews and ongoing training ensured continuous improvement and alignment with business goals.

SIXTEEN

MARASTU®'S SUCCESS WITH A USA TRAVEL WEBSITE

Introduction to the Case Study

In this chapter, we dive into the successful collaboration between Marastu®, an Ahmedabad-based digital marketing agency, and a USA travel website. This story follows Vikas and Rahul from Marastu® as they work closely with Mark and Amelia from the USA travel website to increase mobile app downloads and ticket bookings through a comprehensive performance marketing strategy.

Overview of the Campaign:

Client: USA Travel Website

Objective:

- Increase ticket bookings from their mobile apps and drive more downloads of their mobile app

- Duration: 12 months
- Results: 30% increase in app downloads, 25% increase in user engagement, and 20% increase in ticket bookings

Setting the Stage

Vikas and Rahul, the dynamic duo at Marastu®, were excited about their new client, a well-known travel website in the USA. Mark and Amelia, the marketing leads at the travel website, were keen on boosting their mobile app downloads and increasing ticket bookings through effective digital strategies. They knew they needed a robust performance marketing strategy and were confident that Marastu® was the right partner to achieve their goals.

Initial Meeting:

Mark and Amelia laid out their challenges during the initial meeting. They had a solid user base but struggled with converting website visitors into app users and increasing ticket bookings through the app.

"We need a strategy that combines paid campaigns, social media engagement, SEO, and continuous optimization," said Mark. "We believe Marastu® can help us achieve this," added Amelia.

Vikas and Rahul nodded in agreement, ready to tackle the challenge head-on.

Developing the Strategy

Paid Campaigns:

Vikas, with his extensive experience in paid campaigns, took the lead. "Our first step is to optimize your Google Ads and introduce Bing Ads to tap into a wider audience," he explained.

They identified high-intent keywords for the travel industry, such as "cheap flight tickets," "last-minute travel deals," and "holiday packages." The team created compelling ad copies that highlighted the unique selling points of the travel app, such as exclusive app-only deals and seamless booking experiences.

Case Study:

For example, they targeted users searching for "last-minute travel deals" with an ad showcasing a limited-time offer for app users. This not only drove app downloads but also increased immediate ticket bookings.

Social Media Campaigns

Rahul, an expert in social media marketing, took charge of creating a buzz on platforms like Facebook and Instagram. "We need to engage potential travelers where they spend their time," he said.

They created visually appealing ads featuring beautiful travel destinations, user testimonials, and special app-only promotions. Influencers in the travel space were also engaged to share their experiences using the app, adding a layer of authenticity.

Case Study:

One successful campaign featured an influencer's journey using the app to book a spontaneous weekend getaway. This story, shared across Instagram Stories and Facebook, resulted in a significant spike in app downloads and engagement.

Optimization Techniques

Vikas and Rahul knew that continuous optimization was key to the campaign's success. They implemented a robust A/B testing strategy to refine ad creatives and landing pages.

"We'll test different headlines, images, and CTAs to see what resonates best with our audience," Vikas explained.

Using tools like Google Optimize and Hotjar, they gathered insights into user behavior and identified areas for improvement. Landing pages were optimized for speed and user experience, ensuring a seamless journey from ad click to booking confirmation.

Case Study:

By testing different CTAs, such as "Book Now" versus "Find Your Flight," they discovered that "Book Now" led to a higher conversion rate. Similarly, simplifying the landing page design reduced bounce rates and increased bookings.

Leveraging SEO

Amelia had always believed in the power of SEO but hadn't seen significant results. Rahul assured her, "With the right strategy, we can improve your organic search rankings and drive more traffic to your app."

The team conducted thorough keyword research and optimized the website content for relevant travel-related keywords. They also focused on building high-quality backlinks and creating engaging, informative blog content that catered to travelers' needs.

Case Study:

They created a series of blog posts about top travel destinations, tips for finding cheap flights, and travel itineraries. These posts not only improved search rankings but also provided valuable content that encouraged visitors to download the app for exclusive deals and easier booking.

The Results

After months of hard work and collaboration, the results were clear. Marastu® had successfully helped the USA travel website achieve their goals.

- App Downloads: Increased by 30%
- User Engagement: Increased by 25%
- Ticket Bookings: Increased by 20%

Mark and Amelia were thrilled with the results. "Your team has exceeded our expectations. The app is now a significant driver of our business," Mark said during their final review meeting.

Vikas and Rahul were equally pleased. "It was a team effort, and we're glad we could help you achieve these results," Vikas replied.

Key Takeaways

The success of this campaign can be attributed to several key factors:

Integrated Approach:

Combining paid campaigns, social media engagement, SEO, and continuous optimization ensured a comprehensive strategy that covered all bases.

Data-Driven Decisions:

Regular analysis and optimization based on data insights allowed the team to refine their strategies continuously.

Collaboration and Communication:

Close collaboration between Marastu® and the travel website ensured that everyone was aligned and working towards the same goals.

Innovative Tactics:

Engaging influencers, leveraging A/B testing, and focusing on user experience were crucial in driving app downloads and ticket bookings.

Customer-Centric Focus:

Understanding the needs and behaviors of the target audience allowed the team to create relevant and compelling marketing messages.

Conclusion

The collaboration between Marastu® and the USA travel website showcases the power of a well-executed performance marketing strategy. By focusing on measurable outcomes, leveraging multiple digital channels, and continuously optimizing their efforts, they achieved significant results.

Vikas and Rahul's story is a testament to the importance of teamwork, innovation, and a customer-centric approach in performance marketing. As they continue to help more clients achieve their goals, the lessons learned from this campaign will undoubtedly serve as a blueprint for future success.

A Big Thank You

Thank you for taking the time to read Beyond Clicks: Mastering the Art and Science of Performance Marketing. It has been a pleasure sharing these strategies and insights with you. I am confident that if you apply the strategies mentioned in this book, you can achieve the desired results and elevate your marketing efforts to new heights.

However, always remember that success is not achieved in one go. It is the result of constant and consistent effort, learning, and improvisation. The digital marketing landscape is ever-changing, and staying ahead requires a commitment to continuous improvement and adaptation.

Keep improving, keep learning, and stay dedicated to your goals. I wish you all the great success in your performance marketing journey. Your determination and perseverance will surely lead you to remarkable achievements.

Best of luck,

Vikas Jain